THIS BLOOMSBURY BOOK

BELONGS TO

....

For Katy Gall – queen of all Southport – RC

BLOOMSBURY
CHILDREN'S
BOOKS

First published in Great Britain in 1998 by Bloomsbury Publishing Plc
38 Soho Square, London W1V 5DF

This paperback edition first published 1999

A CIP catalogue record for this book is available from the British Library
ISBN 0 7475 4173 6 (paperback)
ISBN 0 7475 3064 5 (hardback)

Designed by Dawn Apperley
Printed and bound in Belgium by Proost NV, Turnhout

3 5 7 9 10 8 6 4 2

Supposing...

Frances Thomas and Ross Collins

BLOOMSBURY
CHILDREN'S
BOOKS

'Mummy,'
said Little Monster.

'**Supposing** when I
woke up tomorrow morning
... supposing there was a
big ... black ...

l e

in the middle of the floor.

And I didn't want to fall in, so I called you and you didn't answer.

And then supposing the hole got bigger and bigger and it was all dark and smelly.

And then there was a big, big spider and it got closer and closer.

And then there wasn't
a ceiling and the sky was
all horrible and I fell down

and down

and down.

And supposing you couldn't come and help me because you had gone away.

And then the house went on FIRE!

And all the fire was round me when I was falling down the hole.

And the spider was falling too

And I couldn't see the bottom of the hole

And I just went on falling forever and ever and ever.

Mummy, supposing all that happened when I woke up tomorrow, what would it be like?'

'Mmm,' said Mother Monster, 'that would be very scary.

But then supposing tomorrow when you woke up, you called me and I was making pancakes.

And supposing you ate up all your pancakes,

And then we went for a walk.

And supposing we walked and walked until we found a green hill.

And at the bottom of the hill was an old man with a long red scarf, selling balloons.

And supposing I bought a red balloon like a red jewel,

And you bought a green balloon like the green sea,

And a blue balloon
like the blue sky ...'

'And a purple balloon,'
said Little Monster, 'like ...
like a lovely purple balloon.'
'Like a lovely purple balloon,'
said Mother.

'**And** then supposing you and I climbed all the way to the top of the hill, and we stood there in the sun,

And then I let my red balloon float away and away into the sky. And then you let your blue balloon float away and away and your green balloon.'

'Only not my purple balloon,' said Little Monster. 'I would take my purple balloon back home with me.'

'Oh yes,' said Mother Monster. 'We'd take your purple balloon home.

But then on the way we'd
meet an old man with a
long yellow scarf, selling
ice-creams. And supposing
you had strawberry and I
had chocolate ...'

'Or the other way round?' said Little Monster.
'Or the other way round,' said Mother Monster.

'And supposing we walked home eating our ice-creams and just as we'd finished them, it was getting dark, but we got home,

And supposing we went inside and made a fire and toasted some buns ...'

'And you'd tell me a story,' said Little Monster.
'And I'd tell you a story. What would that be like?'
'Mmm,' said Little Monster, 'that would be very nice.'

Then Little Monster said,
'Supposing I took my purple
balloon up to bed with me?
And it floated up to the ceiling
and stayed there ALL NIGHT
and didn't fall down?'
'Mmm,' said Mother.
'That would be very, very nice.'